The Tall T... of Le Sueur

Jason Lee Willis

www.lurapublications.wixsite.com

Library of Congress Cataloging-in-Publication Data
Willis, Jason L., author.
Hawes, Logan J., illustrator.
THE TALL TALE OF LE SUEUR/Jason Lee Willis.-First edition.
Summary: Illustrations accompanied by a poem about a man who comes to the New World for adventures.

ISBN: 979-8-9891198-1-3 (paperback) 979-8-9891198-2-0 (hardcover).
[1. Fiction. 2. Children's fiction. 3. Stories in rhyme. 4. Poetry for children.]
Library of Congress Control Number:

Printed and bound in the United States of America
First Printing October, 2023

Be Warned!

The following story is a tall tale, which means that it is equal parts fact and fiction.

Pierre-Charles Le Sueur was real.
Minnesota is real.
Horned Serpents?
The Philosopher's Stone?
You can be the judge.

T’was 1657 in the land of France
That a giant baby was born
So big he didn’t fit into his pants

“What shall we feed him?”
“What shall we do?”

“We’ll send him to America
Where there’s space and everything’s new.”

So young Pierre Charles Le Sueur
sprang like a deer
Jumping across icebergs
without any fear.

"What a fun adventure!
So much to see!
I'll grow up big in America,
I wonder what I'll be?"

The Jesuits were exploring
out on the frontier.
Le Sueur's arrival
filled them with cheer
"Help us with fishing."
"Help us with camp."
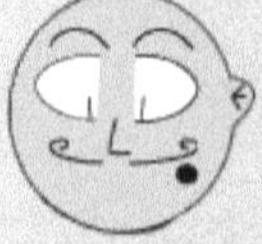
"Lift up our boat
so our robes don't get damp!"

Day after day,
season after season
Le Sueur went outdoors
for any good reason.
He cut down trees
and caught lots of fish.
He got stronger and stronger,
but he had one big wish.

“What’s west of west?
What’s out there to find?
Will the new people I meet

be scary or kind?
Is there wealth?
Or treasure?
Or some lost loot?”
So he put on his suspenders and his best hiking boots

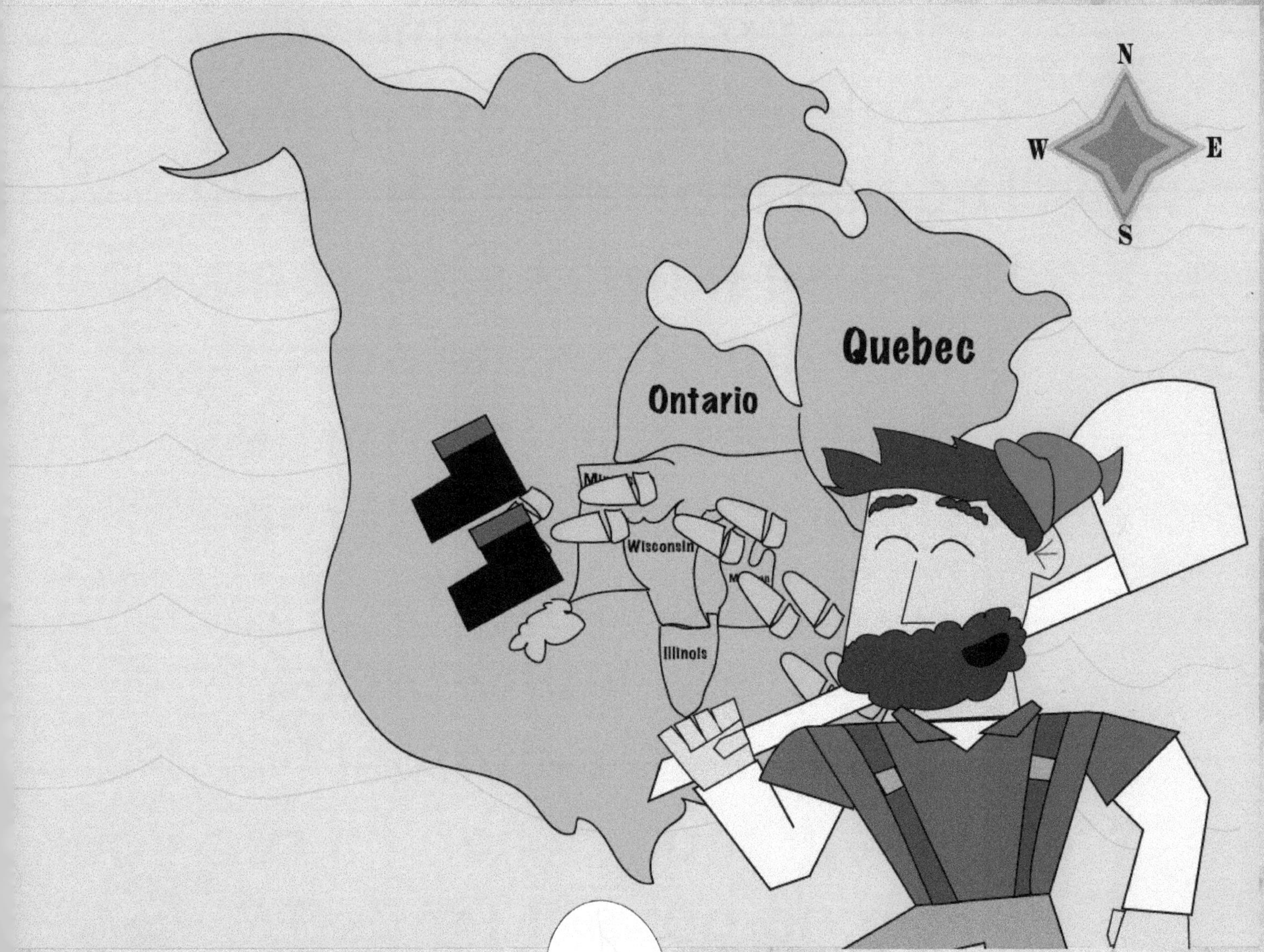
N
W
E
S
Quebec
Ontario
Wisconsin
Illinois

But a problem came up:
people couldn't get along!
They all looked to Le Sueur
because he was so strong.
The English in the south!
The French in the north!
The Iroquois and Huron
all came forth!

"We need some order,
a man we can trust"
Le Sueur agreed, "Then I'll run your
trading post (if I must)."

So Le Sueur ran the trading post,
(it's what he did best)
but his heart still desired
to discover the west.
One day in Wisconsin
while clearing some trees
he heard a voice crying:

"Help me, help me, please."
Her name was Wenonah,
a Dakota from out west
It was love at first sight—
but I'll spare you the rest.

Back at the trading post,
business was booming!
Le Sueur and Wenonah
made quite a team,
but trouble was looming...
Beyond the Mississippi
is where she was from
and never seeing her family
made her quite glum.

Her people were called
the "Seven Council Fires" nation,
and they lived far to the west
of the fur trading station.

"Tun Win is a land
with 10,000 lakes.
The Blue Woman, it is called, and is
why my heart aches."
Wenonah taught him her language
and all about the stars,
but her home was so far away
it felt more distant than Mars.

"I live near the Haunted Valley,
where the earth bleeds blue.
It is guarded by a water monster
with great big horns, too!"

"I'm not afraid of anything,
and I'd really like to see...
the Land of the Blue Woman,
could you please take me?"

Le Sueur traveled more streams and
rivers than he could tally
until Wenonah finally brought him
to the infamous Haunted Valley.

"That is the blue earth,
some think it is magic
If we stay here much longer
the outcome will be tragic!"

They ran into trouble,
(just like she thought)
Wenonah found her lost family,
but Le Sueur got caught.

"Please don't hurt him!
He was nice to me.
Let him go back. Set him free!"
"Our sister is staying,

let's make that clear.
Come back to these lands
and you'll have reason to fear."

Le Sueur left Wenonah
quite broken hearted.
He returned to Montreal,
but a new adventure started.
"I found some weird dirt,

quite strange and blue.
I think it is special, what shall I do?"
"This blue earth is mysterious,
it's something strange to see.
Take it back to France.

Take it across the Sea."

The trip went smoothly,
and he made it to France.
He told the king about the dirt,
and Louis took a chance.
"I'll make you a miner
and give you all you need.
Here are your tools,
you may proceed."

So Le Sueur returned
back across the Atlantic.
When PIRATES appeared!
(He was quite frantic)

The PIRATES were English,
and they took him to a tower.
There he met an alchemist
who had all the power.

"I know your mission.
I caught you blue-handed!
Tell me your secrets
or you will be reprimanded!"
Le Sueur thought of Wenonah,
who he really missed,
and kept his secrets away
from the English scientist.

While Le Sueur was stuck in prison, the guys in Montreal kept trying to find the place with blue earth, but without Le Sueur, they kept dying!

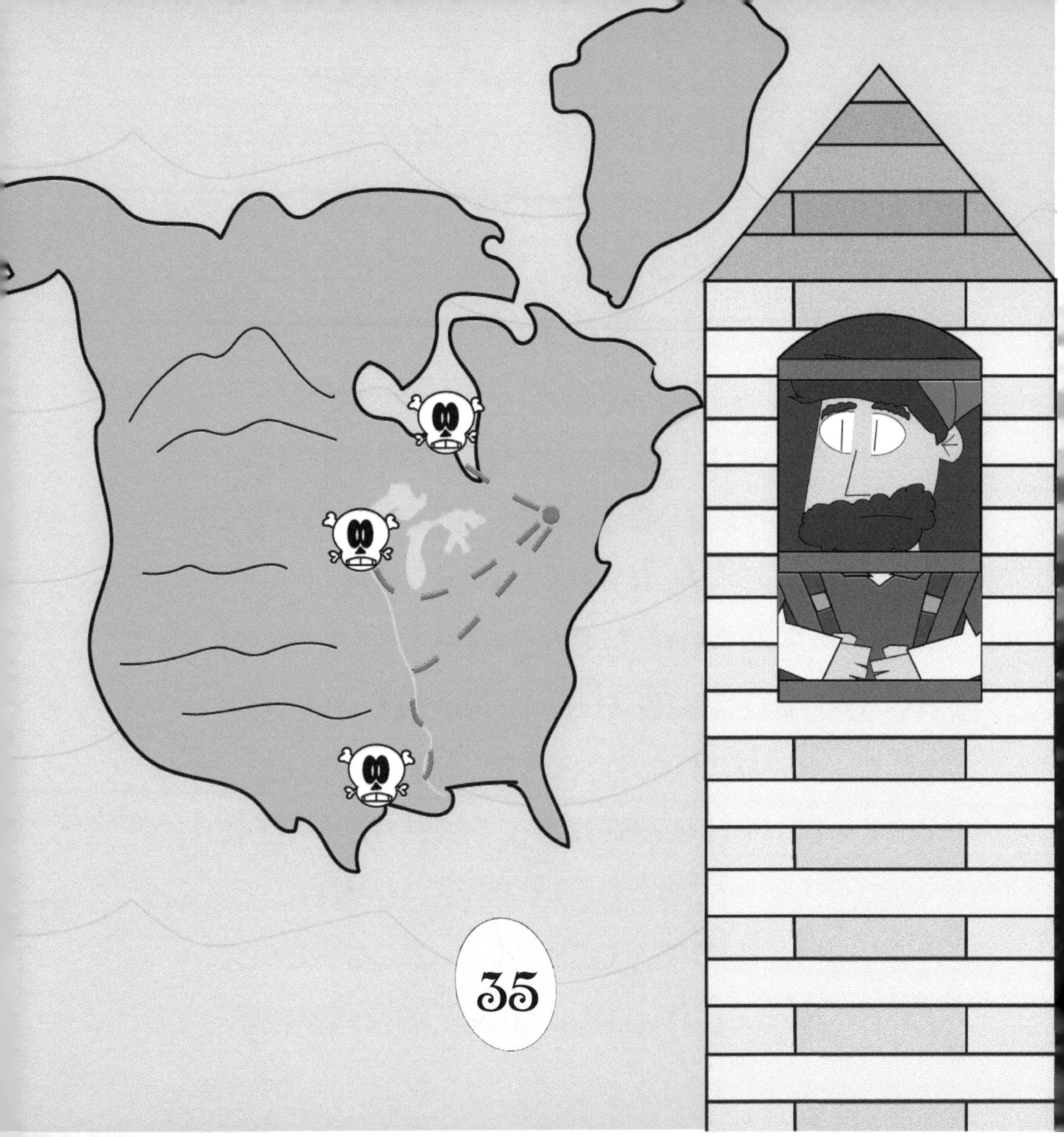

Back in his tower,
Le Sueur was quite amazed.
The strange scientist
was entirely crazed.
"I analyzed your blue earth,
and copper it's not!

So I did some reading
to see what we've got.
A long time ago,
a great treasure was lost,
and scientists have been searching for
it, no matter the cost.
The treasure creates vitriol,
that part is known.
I think you've discovered
the Philosopher's Stone."

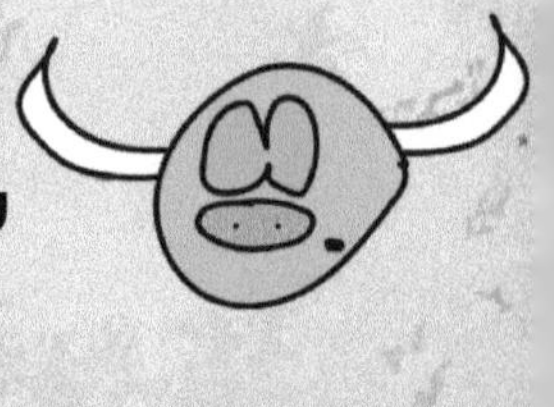

The treasure I seek is more important

than England and France.
By releasing you
at least we've got a chance.
Instead of returning west,
you'll be sent south.
To the mighty Mississippi
(we discovered it's mouth).

You'll get a new ship
and be set free.
Go dig up the stone
and return it to me!"

Le Sueur was happy,
and up the river he went!
But a team of friends and enemies
were also sent.
Le Sueur was the leader
since he knew the way,
and he and his miners
paddled day after day.

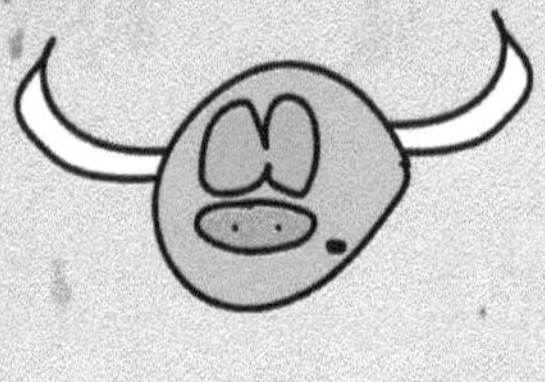

Sneaking in south,
behind Wenonah's brothers,
Le Sueur would had left the miners
(if he had his druthers).
But a promise is a promise,
and he had one to keep,
So he risked his life to return
to the valley so deep.
"Here is the vitriol. Dig up your dirt.

But make it snappy
so we don't get hurt."

But before they could dig
the wind began to blow
and covered the Haunted Valley
with FOUR FEET of snow!
"Oh, shoot, it looks like we're stuck!

We'll be here all winter.
It's certainly bad luck."

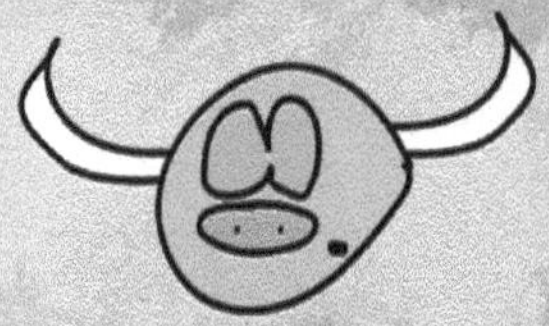

Luckily for the miners,
Le Sueur was quite bold.
He built them a wooden fort
to protect them from the cold.
He cooked them warm food,
(buffalo-on-a-stick),
and he hoped that his kindness
might do the trick.

Fort Blue Bull was built quickly,
(Le Sueur was not lazy).
but then Wenonah's cousins showed
up, asking "Are you crazy?

Tear this all down,
and leave the Haunted Valley.
Your lives are in danger!
Hurry, don't dally."

"Rich men sent me here,
including the king.
I'll let them do the digging
and leave in the Spring."

FORT BLUE BULL

When the snow finally melted,
the miners got right to work.
Le Sueur worried about digging there
(he felt like a jerk).
The miners dug deep
and made a hole that was large.
They packed up the vitriol
and put it in a barge.

FORT BLUE BUL

At the bottom of the pit,
they found something white.
It looked kinda strange,
it was an unexpected sight.
“What is it, what is it?”
One of the miners wondered.
“Finders keepers,” said another,
“This mine will be plundered!”

Then everyone started fighting
To take hold of the strange treasure.
Even Le Sueur got involved,
which gave him great pleasure.
The white stone is mine,
everyone was saying.
When in reality...
they should have been praying.
Wenonah's brother had come
and heard all the noise,
So he quickly gathered up
all of the boys.

FORT BLUE BULL

The Dakota had found them
and caught them blue-handed.
They were stuck far from home.
In fact, they were stranded.
Wenonah's brothers were angry;
they were filled with fury.
But Wenonah knew the strangers
and served as the jury.

FORT BLUE BULL

Le Sueur explained everything
and how he'd been sent
to collect a special treasure
(and for another chance to see her),
he went.

"I'm glad you came to see me,
but you really must know...
my brothers are really angry,
And so you must go."

So what became of the treasure?
That was called the philosopher's stone?
The end of this story
is not entirely known.
Did he give it to Wenonah
for her to protect and keep?
Or did he bring it to the Atlantic
and throw it in the deep?
Did the miners take it and bring it back to France?
Or did he return to the tower
and make the scientist dance?

What we do know is that LeSueur left
And sailed back down the river.
With a load of blue earth
and scary stories
that would make a Frenchman shiver.

Stories of Le Sueur became legendary:
how he roamed through the big woods
and out onto the prairie.
Is Le Sueur the reason
we have stories of "Tall Paul"
Or did writers simply invent it all?
Le Sueur was so big
he could surely break a scale,
but that's why his life
was perfect for a tall tale.

Tale of
Tall Paul

That's the end of the story.
There's nothing left to tell!
This page is just the credits
for guys who make books to sell.

If the pictures made you ponder and pause... they were made by a guy named Logan J. Hawes

If you liked rhyming and the lizard cordylus... this book was written by Jason Lee Willis

Milton Keynes UK
Ingram Content Group UK Ltd.
UKHW051221181223
434575UK00008B/71

9 798989 119813